Prince Iridescent
and the cloudy day

By
Hope LaVelle

Illustrated by
Patrizia Diana

All inquiries should be directed to HopeForHire.com

The characters, places, and events in this book are fictitious.
Any similarity to a real person, place, or thing is purely coincidental and not intended by the author.

Text by Hope LaVelle
Illustrations, Cover, and Interior Design by Patrizia Diana
Registered with the Library of Congress
ISBN (hardcover) 979-8-9898996-0-9
ISBN (softcover) 979-8-9898996-1-6
ISBN (ebook) 979-8-9898996-2-3
Library of Congress Control Number: 2024901402

for

MAMA BEAR

from your Darling Daughter

In the kingdom of Prismatica, the land of color and light,
Princess Iridescent reigns over this beautiful sight.

The creatures adore her and run free with glee,
all of them so colorful, and bright as can be.

But one day, to all the creatures' surprise,
dark clouds rolled in, covering the sun and the sky.

The color of Prismatica suddenly turned a dull gray,
"Princess Iridescent! Can you make those clouds go away?"

The creatures pleaded as they worried with fright.
All the color was gone, and so was the light!

The Princess saw someone float down to her castle.
Perhaps this someone was the cause of this hassle.

"I am King Cloudius, King of the Clouds,
and all of your color is just too loud!

I've come to take over your kingdom today.
You're all too happy, I like it more gray."

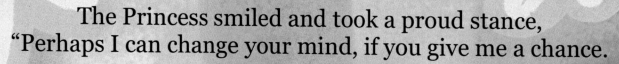

The Princess smiled and took a proud stance,
"Perhaps I can change your mind, if you give me a chance.

I'll show how beautiful life is with color,
maybe then you won't want this land to be duller."

"Ha! You can try, but I won't be swayed.
Then I'll make the whole kingdom this
permanent shade."

The Princess took him on a walk through her garden,
but this just made his expression harden.

"Do you like the way the flowers dance in the breeze?"
"I do not like it one bit," said the King with ease.

"Do you like the way the elefly flutters?"
"No, I do not," King Cloudius muttered.

Princess Iridescent took him into the woods.
If anything could convince him, this surely would.

"I think you'll like all these beautiful trees."
"Think again, silly Princess," the King disagreed.

"The crystals shine with every color we know,
and the mushrooms sparkle whenever they grow."

"What's the big deal? It's nothing that neat.
Now show me the throne and I'll take a seat."

But the Princess wasn't done trying her best.
She had much more to put to the test.

"How about the fairy fish and how they glow?"
And for a moment the King grinned,
but you'd never know.

"Our turtlebugs are the kindest creature,
and the rainbow waterfall is our favorite feature!"

King Cloudius' eyes grew big at the view,
but he then shook his head, and quickly withdrew.

And, finally, she took him to the top of the hill,
to view the whole kingdom.
The King grew still.

"I hate it! I HATE IT! It's just not fair!
You get to make color, and I make despair."

Suddenly,
as King Cloudius began to yell,
thunder rumbled and roared,
and then the rain fell.

"My life is always so gray and so bland.
I'm jealous of your color, your sunshine, and land!

I'll never be able to make something so pretty,
so I'll sit here, pout, and be petty."

The rain fell down hard as he cried about gray.
But, once he was done huffing and puffing,
the clouds fell away.

The Princess smiled and tapped Cloudius politely,
"Look what you've made, it shines so brightly!"

King Cloudius sniffled and looked up through his tears,

to see a rainbow so colorful, so bright and so clear!

"I made that?" asked the King with surprise.

"You sure did! That's all yours!
As you can see with your eyes.

Everyone has power to bring color to the world."
The Princess explained as King Cloudius twirled.

The King could not hold back a laugh and a grin,
"Alright you got me, looks like you win."

Princess Iridescent smiled and said,
"Looks like you won something better instead."

And with that,
King Cloudius said goodbye,
hopped on his cloud,
and flew back to the sky.

All the kingdom rejoiced and cheered for the Princess,
as the color returned to its full glory and brightness.

About the Author

Hope LaVelle

Growing up with no self-confidence, Hope LaVelle always
wanted to find a way to let her true colors shine.
It was through storytelling that Hope found her voice,
and went on to make award winning stories that make people
laugh, cry, and feel inspired.
She continues to spread positivity through entertainment, and shares
magical worlds that encourage kindness, imagination, and, of course,
color!

Made in the USA
Middletown, DE
01 October 2024